SAWYER BECKETT'S GUIDE FOR ~~FOOLS~~ *Tools*

LOOKING TO DATE MY DAUGHTER

Sawyer Beckett's Guide for ~~Fools~~ Tools Looking to Date My Daughter

©2016 S.E. Hall

Cover Design: Ramie Kerschen

Editor: Misty Lingle

Proofing by Jill Sava

Formatter: Brenda Wright, Formatting Done Wright

Thank you all!

"They say from the instant he lays eyes on her, a father adores his daughter. Whoever she grows up to be, she is always to him that little girl in pigtails. She makes him feel like Christmas. In exchange, he makes a secret promise not to see the awkwardness of her teenage years, the mistakes she makes or the secrets she keeps."

— Unknown

Table of Contents

It has come to my attention, kinda like being smacked in the face by a fucking 2x4, that my daughter is either suffering from hallucinations, (it'd be frowned upon for me to actually root for that being the case, right?), or *thinks* she's old enough to date. And no, we're not talking about the days of some shaky lil' boy coming to my door so his parents can drive him and my angel to the chaperoned school dance, both his folks waving from the car with shit-eating grins on their yuppie faces, 'cause they know the same thing I do — they have a son, ONE penis to worry about, but I have a daughter, EVERY penis to worry about... and how to cut it off without getting caught. *Nooooo*, Miss Priss, despite my best efforts, went and figured out how to grow up. She's now not only living on her own, but has somehow translated her age and the fact she has an apartment into some imaginary, golden ticket to freedom that allows her to go out whenever she wants, to who the hell knows where and do who the hell knows what, with friends (many of which are *male*) that I didn't even know existed!

It's a full-time job just keeping what few tabs I do have on her, and now this "oh yeah Dad, I run around and date" bullshit.

I need more guns.

I don't see her at breakfast every morning anymore. I don't know what outfit she found, *mistakenly*, appropriate to wear each day. And I definitely no longer have the chance to tuck her into bed every night, hanging on every word of the innocent, little girl babble of what Suzy said to Tommy on the playground that day.

And now, just another "surprise" discovery that reinforces what I've been telling myself isn't true — I'm still losing her a little more each day.

Not gonna lie — it hurts like a motherfucker.

Last time I checked though, she's not thirty yet, nor am I dead, and I'm pretty fuckin' positive those were the strict stipulations to her ever dating, that I've recited at least once a day, every day, since... well, since she was old enough to understand what I was saying. So I'll be damned if I go down without a fight.

But *some* people, (everyone in The Crew, all of whom I'm *this* close to throwing overboard), say I'm being ridiculous and fooling myself by thinking I have any say-so left in the matter. I've always been the best looking *and* smartest one in the group, so I'm not sure why I'm even listening to them. Oh that's right, because they won't shut the hell up! So in the interest of their silence, and of course compromise, because it's another well-known fact that I'm a reasonable, level-headed guy — I'm going to give all you horny, piss-ant lil' fuckers sniffing around my daughter a fighting chance.

A very slim chance.

(And it's really for one reason only... I don't want Princess P to get mad and give me that "controlling tyrant" speech of hers again. Plus, she tells me a lot more when she's *not* not talking to me.)

Don't get too excited yet you bastards. I'm not having your ass over for dinner to "get to know ya" or anything else just as asinine. No, the only scrap of assistance you're gonna get is this manual. Way I figure, at least twenty percent of you "dead punks walking" can't read. Another fifty percent of you will get scared and disappear out of the picture. Which leaves thirty, just thirty percent of you lil' bastards, *at best*, that *might* make it to the final cut.

I'm likin' my odds.

And, I'll be able to smile, guilt-free, when I tell my baby girl that I tried.

So, let's get this party started.

The most important thing for you to know is this: your first "date" *will be with me*. If and when you've read this entire survival guide, yes, emphasis on survival — your own — you still insist on pursuing my daughter, you and I will have ourselves a "sit down."

Be sure and bring a notebook and number two pencil with you to this *meeting*, because it's not gonna be some friendly chat over a burger and a few beers. You, naïve glutton for punishment that you are, will be quizzed over all the guidelines I'm about to school you on... under bright lights, and allowed nothing to drink for that nervous, cottonmouth thing ya got goin' on, which works out perfectly with the fact you'll also be denied any bathroom breaks until we're done. Unless of course you piss down your leg, which you very well may.

Anything less than a 100% on said quiz will be considered a FAIL, and you will be escorted from my property immediately, in a manner of my choosing. And before you ask, *fuck no* there aren't any re-tests or opportunities for extra credit, and no way in hell do I grade on a curve.

Ya know what? You should probably just stop reading right now and go find some other girl with a dumbass dad you might stand a chance against. I won't think any less of you, I'm not the judgmental type. Actually, this very wise decision would tell me you at least have somewhat of a brain... the one in the head on top of your neck, and you're finally using it.

Atta' boy!

But, should you decide to proceed... let the games begin!

Surprise, surprise — once again, Daney, "Mr. McWorryLikeAPuss" has insisted I include a "cover my ass" clause. Some shit about guys who have, or are currently, (I'd say you're as good as dead if either's the case, but apparently that defeats the purpose of the upcoming disclaimer), dating my daughter could possibly whine like a titbag that I'm issuing threats against them.

~~I AM!~~

Can't say that either.

So here ya go. I'll give you three guesses who wrote this part... and the first two don't count.

DISCLAIMER: This handbook is for entertainment purposes only, directed at no actual person(s). It's simply one father's thoughts and opinions when it comes to his daughter dating. No young men were harmed, physically or otherwise, held against their will and/or interrogated during the making of this fictional work, nor is it suggested or encouraged in any way that any fathers who happen to read this try anything contained herein at home.

Or anywhere.

On anyone.

There, now Daney can calm his tits and I can get on with it — the regulations to know like the back of your hand if you're even thinking about *thinking about* dating my daughter.

And again, any of you dads out there who do buy up a bunch of copies and start handing 'em out to your own daughters' potential boyfriends, just remember... I put in a disclaimer. So make sure you tell your daughters and/or wives not to come bitchin' at me for bail money.

And to the young men reading — I assure you, when it comes to a little girl's daddy, no matter how old she may be, it's a helluva lot easier to work *with* us than against us.

Especially if that daddy is me.

Don't say I didn't warn ya, *toolbag.*

Sawyer Beckett's Guide for ~~Fools~~ Tools Looking to Date My Daughter

RULE #1:
Secrets

You no longer have any.

We're starting here because if you're lookin' to date my girl, then I'm lookin' for each and every skeleton in any closet you've ever hung a shirt in, boy. And you better not be hidin' any doozies. If you are, no need to read beyond this point. I *will* find out, every speck of dirt there is to know about you. You see, I've got this certain friend, who even scares the shit out of me with the Intel he has — man already knows or can find out anything, about anyone, in a matter of time so quick that it reeks of mafia ties he's failed to mention.

Sawyer Beckett's Guide for ~~Fools~~ Tools Looking to Date My Daughter

The terms "sealed record" or "expunged" have no meaning in his world, so keep that in mind.

And of course I'll be talking to your buddies... especially when I can catch 'em out drinking. That's when they'll be loose-lipped and tell me everything I want to know. *And*, I'll see their true colors. Who you run with says a lot about you — you hang with stray dogs, you have fleas.

But as I've mentioned, I'm a rational man, so I'm not gonna *purposely* dig up every time you acted like the jackass you are and tell my daughter. (Although, how much fuckin' fun would that be?) But honestly, I don't care about that time you thought it was just a fart and some shit came out or when you couldn't handle all the *wine coolers* your friends made you drink and when you passed out first, they drew a dick on your face.

Those aren't "secrets." They're just proof you're a dumbass, which I already knew.

No, I'm hunting for the things in your past that fall into two categories: "Oh, *Hell* No" and "I'll Give You 30 Seconds to Explain."

Yes, I'll define them for you. *Jesus, you need me to shit and piss for ya too?*

The "Hellllllllll NOs" are the following, and/or anything close:

*Any jail time.

*Your fingerprints on file in any system other than for application into the military.

*Ever being brought in by the police for questioning on ANY matter.

*Ever being asked to participate in a line-up. (Even if they didn't pick your ass; if you were in the line, you're done here.)

Sawyer Beckett's Guide for ~~Fools~~ Tools Looking to Date My Daughter

*Any kids you're hiding and/or not taking the utmost care of. (Nope, I don't care if DNA was done or not; I find one woman who says it's yours, it's yours. And if you didn't introduce your child, proudly, to my daughter or at least tell her right off the bat — you're out. *AND*, if you're not providing for that child, go start doing so NOW, you worthless piece of shit.)

*Any ex-wives. (Save your "annulment" or "drunk in Vegas" speeches. It counts.)

*Any complaints ever filed against you by a female. (If I find one, I'm gonna beat your ass to teach you a lesson. And because I can.)

I reserve the right to add to this list at any time, without prior notice, or even a reason. Because I can.

If you qualified for any above item — get the fuck gone. Fast. Like you're being chased by a large, angry father. Because you are.

If, by some miracle, you made it through these cuts, feel free to keep reading. But pay careful attention... you're not out of the woods yet by any means.

So you made it this far, which only tells me you're not a hardened criminal; your parents must be so proud. But anything else "sketchy" in your history — you need to fess up to me before I find out on my own. Little things, that may seem insignificant to you, aren't. They're a big deal to me, and they grow even bigger every second you try to hide them. These, what I'll generously refer to as "minor" offenses, are the ones you have 30 seconds to explain.

*Speeding/parking tickets/any traffic violations in general. These are important and need to be carefully scrutinized by me because I'll be damned if your irresponsible, reckless ass is gonna be driving my baby girl around, all hopped up on adrenaline and bad decision-making skills. We can work on this one though. (God, I'm such a giver.) I'm willing to donate unselfishly of my time and take you out for my special brand of a driving lesson. I'm lookin' forward to it really. However, my daughter, the most precious thing in the world to me, is not to go on any rides with you behind the wheel until this happens. And I can't wait to see what you drive. It better not be some lil' rice-burner, wind-up toy car where every vehicle on the highway is bigger than you... obviously posing hazards that worry me even more than thinking about you driving.

And if all else fails, because you're too far gone and can't be re-trained and/or drive a Matchbox car, we'll just establish the rule that my angel, who was taught by the best, will always be the one to drive, her car... while you and your mangina ride passenger. Should this stipulation have to be put in place, I know my P, and she will now think you're either a pussy, you actually *have* a pussy, you're same-sex oriented or will promptly place you in the friend zone. Problem solved!

*Cheating. Of any sort. And before you get all cocky and think you can easily handle this one, let me tell you what "cheating" means in my dictionary. Anything you wouldn't do if my daughter, *or myself*, were watching is cheating. Yeah — shit just got real. I'll track down every teacher you're ever had, every test you've ever taken and every girl you've ever so much as texted. You're gonna want to delete your Facebook, SnapChat, Instagram and Tinder accounts right about now. And I still may find 'em.

If deceit is *embedded* in your nature, like I find you cheated on lots of tests and/or girls, not just once or twice when you were very young, then we have two options. Electric shock therapy to untangle the wire in your brain that thinks cheating is okay is our first, and my personal, choice.

Or, you can forget my daughter's name and get lost. I stand corrected; this one may be my preference.

*Fighting. Again, gonna find everyone from your fucking pre-school teachers, your camp counselors, to your coaches... no rock (out from under which you crawled) unturned. This particular category can either ruin you or work in your favor. You see, there's a fine line between being able to kick some ass when you're hit first or defending a lady and being a hot-head. If I find that you're the latter, a cocky punk with a short temper — I'm sending ya packin'.

I reserve the right to add to *this* list at any time too.

So secrets… I think you get my drift. If not, you're too damn dumb to date my daughter anyway. If you *are* able to keep up so far and think your "rap sheet" will pass inspection, have your confessional list prepared when you arrive to our lil' pow-wow.

On a side note, you should also bring your best attempt at a real man's handshake. While I proceed to shake just short of snapping every tiny, fragile bone that makes up the human hand — yours in this case- you are expected to bear down and take it without so much as a flinch. If you squeeze back, bonus point. But if you wince, whimper, dare to try to pull away or cry — which wouldn't surprise me a damn bit — your visit is over. Take your sorry, limp-wristed ass home. You've been disqualified.

Not to mention disgraced.

Sawyer Beckett's Guide for ~~Fools~~ Tools Looking to Date My Daughter

You just let out a huge sigh of relief, didn't you? You're thinking, "it's not that bad, I can handle this no problem."

Ah, that's precious, *Nancy*.

Well *now*, take a deep breath in and return immediately to the state of 'scared shitless' you were in — and will remain in — for the duration of your half-cocked plan to be any part of my daughter's life. Because this is an *ongoing* investigation, boy. I'm not just wading through the cobwebs in your closet once. No, no, no... I already have all the apps installed on my phone to continually check your shit, including the county jail intake website, and a standing reservation with an officer, who shall remain nameless, to know, on the daily, if you so much as slow-roll through a stop sign.

And I'm gonna shake your hand the same way every damn time I see you.

Be afraid. *Stay* Afraid.

RULE #2:
Curfew

Let's clear up any misconceptions you might have about this right now. SHE. HAS. ONE.

I know what you're thinking. Stop. If I trusted *your* thinking, I wouldn't need to write you a manual, now would I?

The word "curfew" has gotten a raw deal — young people such as yourself have made their own adaptations to its definition. This isn't the urban dictionary punk, so I looked it up in the old school dictionary for ya.

Curfew: *noun; Middle English word origin.* A regulation requiring people to remain indoors between specified hours, typically at night.

Granted, some of the examples offered do mention the word "parents" — which is fine by me, cause guess what — I'm *still* her parent, no matter how old she gets. But nowhere, not even in those lil' *unhelpful* "let's use it in a sentence" hints that you foolishly think contain your escape clause, does it specify a starting or ending age for curfew enforcement.

Therefore, twenty-five or fifty-five... SHE. HAS. ONE.

You ever heard the saying "nothing good happens after midnight?" Yeah, it's not "nothing good happens to people under eighteen after midnight." There's a reason for that. Drunk drivers and degenerates don't discriminate based on age. Neither do emergency rooms.

God did not bless me with my beautiful, amazing child for her to close down the bars or tip the third-shift waitress at IHOP. He, and I, have a far bigger purpose for her life in mind. And if you care about her... so do you.

Now at first, I was going to set the curfew at one a.m. But then, one of the coolest women I know popped in my head, and I'm not too proud to admit, her "Disney Defense," which she can find a way to apply to *any* real-life situation, made sense to me.

Cinderella had to be home at midnight, and even then, poor girl lost a shoe and had to wobble her way home on one foot, with only some mice, a couple horses and a pretty tired lookin' dog to protect her.

So even midnight is iffy, but I figure if it worked out for one princess, I'm willing to allow it for *my* princess.

Midnight it is, boy. I'd explain to you where the little and big hand are pointing at that time, but since we both know you're gonna check your phone — that's a digital reading of "12:00 AM."

Not "ish." There's no fucking "ish" in this rule. Not 12:01, none of that "well, we left the place at twelve" bullshit you're already planning to spew at me. What I'm saying to you is — my daughter is to be inside her apartment at midnight, with the door locked and your ass on the *other* side of it. You *are* to walk her to the door, make sure she gets inside safely, but you don't step one toe over the threshold.

Has this put a dent in your plans? Not sounding like as much fun to date a girl you must have home this early? You're absolutely right! (Savor that, it's not something I'm likely to ever say again.) I wouldn't blame you a bit if you wanted to call this whole thing off right now.

Sawyer Beckett's Guide for ~~Fools~~ Tools Looking to Date My Daughter

Oh, and one last thing. Being the kind and generous person I am, which we've clearly established multiple times already, I'm gonna let you have all the credit on this one. Meaning — this was *your* idea when my daughter asks, most likely in a whiney "you're no fun" voice, why you're taking her home so early.

Deal with it, like a man... and keep my name out your mouth.

You throw me under the bus and I'll throw you six feet under.

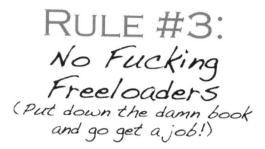

RULE #3:
No Fucking Freeloaders
(Put down the damn book and go get a job!)

If you've made it this far and are still confident that you have a snowball's chance in my form of Hell, then either you're *wrong* (that's where I'm putting my money) or you're employable.

So you best be employed.

Being "employed" doesn't mean you work a few hours here and there on the weekends for one of your "bros" and/or family members. Selling your old shit on Ebay, Craigslist or to your local pawn shop when you need cash — also not a job. And it *damn* sure doesn't mean you grow pot in your closet and "distribute" it,

and/or sell off your prescription medications that you
"don't think you need anymore."

In fact, if you *do* have any prescriptions, bring
those with you to our meeting too. And yes, now that
I've thought of it, I'll be checking on the history of this
too. No, HIPPA can't save you; remember the scary,
possibly mob-tied friend I mentioned? Yep, he'll get me
the info. (Please refer back in your handbook to the
section titled "Secrets" and my right to add to that list at
any time. I just did.)

"Employed" needs to look something like this:

A forty hour a week job that requires you to
report to a well-established company that has a public
building, *with a sign and everything*, from which you
receive a steady paycheck, *AND* the establishment is
recognized as existent by the Better Business Bureau.

If you are a full-time student — and honestly, if I have to tell you that this doesn't mean *one* online course, you're fucking hopeless — I am willing to keep an open-mind to amending the above requirements, when you present to me your current class schedule. (Which I'll have already obtained myself, so they better match!)

But even if we get all this worked out, I'll still expect to see proof that you have money in your wallet, by means that do NOT include:

*Given to you by your parents. My daughter works *and* goes to school, you can too. Figure it out! (No silver-spoon, privileged tit boys that couldn't fix my princess's flat tire allowed.)

*Anything illegal. Don't think I was kidding before about your prescriptions or precious pot plants. Searching your closets was literal and figurative.

Sawyer Beckett's Guide for ~~Fools~~ Tools Looking to Date My Daughter

*Any activity where the words stripper, pimp or "I don't know his real name" come up. I own a club, so I'm okay with you bartending, bouncing or being a DJ, but not at a strip club where pimps and dealers run their businesses from the back room. And if there's a certain hallway where every door has a light above it, able to switch from "occupied red" to "open for use green," get the fuck out of here. But if you do, in fact, work at a club that you think is good enough to pass inspection, go ahead and plan on giving me a tour. I'll surprise you for that — a "pop in" — it'll be fun. As if I'd let you "offer" to take me in the middle of the day when nothing's happening and everyone's been warned I'm coming. Nice try.

Right about now you're probably wondering what prescriptions *I'm* on, or should be on, since I'm coming off like an overprotective lunatic.

Thing is- I AM an overprotective lunatic, and I don't give a damn who knows it. I kick ass at every job I have, and my number one job is being P's dad.

I figured out a long time ago, I never have to count the dollars if I count every cent. Yes, I realize I just lost you. What I mean is, if I lay out every single thing, big or small, for you now, I don't have to worry about being blindsided by some huge issue down the road.

Dear God, still confused, fucktard? How's this... if I watch every penny, I never wake up one day to find I don't even have a dollar. Hear me now?

Then hear this too — my daughter doesn't do "dutch," nor is she ever going to be asked to "spot you a twenty." Never will she be sitting at home, waiting for you to get off "work" where you stared at other naked women on a pole all night. And she'll never have to worry about what happens if your Daddy cuts you off, or

God forbid, "tragedy strikes," and your marijuana plants die.

Because I've already safe-guarded her against any of those possibilities. I counted the cents.

Still think you're good enough? That you can handle it?

Well then by all means, turn the page schmuck.

RULE #4:
Taking Her Out— EVERYONE is the Enemy.

Of course you'll be taking her out; to dinner, movies that *she* wants to see, and I'm sure, as much as I hate it, the occasional club or party... because I know she loves to dance. Tried everything, couldn't change her mind on that worrisome habit. I'm willing to try and accept this though, because as we've established, your ass better not be broke, bumming your way through a cheap date of movies and take-out on her couch. "Netflix and Chill" is *not* an option! You won't even know what her couch looks like you sorry lil' — never mind, we'll get to that.

So back to Rule Four: Going out in public.

Sawyer Beckett's Guide for ~~Fools~~ Tools Looking to Date My Daughter

Obviously, you've seen my daughter, or you wouldn't be sniffin' around with your tail waggin'. Well guess what? Everyone else can see her too. Welcome to my world, I've been ready to kill every guy in every place we've gone to since she was thirteen years old.

Never let your guard down. I don't care if you're at church, you need to start practicing your new way of thinking in every situation, even the "safe" ones... that way having your guard up and eyes wide open will become a habit. *Everyone* is a predator, just waiting for that moment you leave her alone, turn your head, or get drunk and sloppy.

Do you have a little sister? I hope so; 'cause I want you to think about each and every worry you'd have if she went, to say... a frat party. Now, use all those awful thoughts running through your mind as fuel to guide you anytime my daughter's safety is in your hands.

And while you're at it — go drag your sister outta the frat party; what the fuck is wrong with you?

As added reinforcement, I've purchased all seasons of *Law and Order: SVU* for you on DVD. It's my wife's favorite show, and watching it with her over the years has scarred me for life, yes, but in a productive way — it's taught me all the possible scenarios I'm now schooling you on.

*Crowds. When it comes to packed places in which there are *any* other men, could be one, could be one-hundred, ASSUME THE WORST.

My daughter is a smart girl and Lord knows I've drilled it into her head her entire life that you can never be too careful, but it's not *her* behavior or decisions I worry about — it's everyone else's. That now, and foremost, includes *yours*.

*Drinks. If you didn't make it yourself or watch it being made like a hawk, then deliver it straight to her hand, never taking your eyes off of it 'til the cup was empty — IT IS SPIKED. You know what? You go ahead and take a drink of it first anyway, regardless of all stipulations above. Wait ten minutes. If you're not dizzy or dead, you may proceed to hand it to her — *eyes still don't leave the glass!* I'd insist we stick to a "you pop the top on sealed bottle or can" rule, but we both know girls always want the colorful, fruity shit that comes in a glass. *Can't make anything easy on me.*

*Bathroom Breaks. Neither of you are ever to take one alone again. If she needs to go, you escort her, swing the door wide open, have her pause before entering to confirm no one is lurking inside and then your ass does not move from right outside that door 'til she reemerges.

I'm not just "winging" it on my crazy with this one; statistics prove that eight out of ten attackers will nab you right when you walk in or out of the door, so again — swing that fucker open like you're trying to kill anything on the other side of it.

Yeah, people will look at you like you've lost your mind. Fun fact — through the years, between all the kids in our "Crew," their various ball games, and their extensive training on this matter, my friends and I have had to deal with many an angry parent because one of our kids knocked their kid out with a flying bathroom door.

Better safe than sorry.

Now if *you're* the one who has to go — hold it.

Yes, I'm dead fucking serious.

You're not "leaving her with the group" while you go take a leak, and she's damn sure not waiting outside the door in a dark hallway *or* going in a guy's stanky-ass bathroom with you, random dudes with their junk hanging out in front of her. So like I said — HOLD IT.

Separating. Suppose my girl says, "Oh, I see so and so over there, I'm gonna go say hi. I'll be right back." I'm not even going to tell you the answer on this one. If your head isn't already shaking in agreement with me while you read this, mentally listing all the reasons this is a *terrible* idea, you've learned NOTHING and we're DONE.

You no longer have to concern yourself with learning how to hold your urine, flinging open doors like a lunatic or staying in "Secret Service" form at funerals because YOU FAIL!

Dancing. She wants to go out on the floor with her friends? I don't care if you look like you're having a seizure when you attempt to dance, you get your uncoordinated ass out there, *right* beside her and bounce your fucking shoulders a little or some shit. If you let her get caught up in the mosh pit of "oops" hands and "accidental" body parts bumping — I will kill you.

By this point, you stand a very good chance of being called "clingy" or "suffocating." But *real* men can easily turn that into "protectively attractive." Not too attractive! I'm not training you on how to get some play, Asshat! I'm simply giving you a warning out of the kindness of my heart... because you're not allowed to blame any of this on me either.

*Making your way home. Don't be a tight ass, use valet anytime it's available. Thus, eliminating the need for you to go get the car while my child waits, unguarded. And I'm not crazy about the idea of you traipsing across a dark parking lot, even together, either — so use valet.

Sawyer Beckett's Guide for ~~Fools~~ Tools Looking to Date My Daughter

If there's no valet service at whatever hole in the wall you've decided it's wise to drag my daughter to, park close to the door, under a light and have your key positioned in your hand to strike and stab with it. (My girl already knows this trick, so maybe you should hand her the key; she's highly trained in the art of stabby.)

*When you get home. Let's start with the most vital part of this rule first — YOUR HORNY ASS IS NOT STAYING. Remember when I said you won't even know what her couch looks like? This is what I was talking about. You see her to the door, *don't forget to swing that motherfucker wide open if P doesn't do it first,* make sure she gets inside and a few lights turned on, wait, *on the doorstep,* for her to check for anyone inside or signs of a break-in. When she comes back and tells you it's all good, turn around, get in your car and go the fuck home. And when you get there, call and check on her.

I know you're wondering... if I'm this paranoid, how is she even living outside my home in the first place? Who was watching her like a hawk up to now?

The answer to your first question is... my Princess has a mother. A mother who insisted I "let up" a little, and coincidentally, is the same woman I enjoy having sex with and/or at least have her speaking to me.

The second answer is... me, you shriveled up nutsack. *Me.*

I had the alarm system installed on her place. *I* call my baby girl multiple times a day and know her routine by heart. *I* make a habit to know all her friends and everything about them; hell, I helped raise the best of them. So you see, we have a pattern in place that was just starting to give me some comfort... until you came along.

Sawyer Beckett's Guide for ~~Fools~~ Tools Looking to Date My Daughter

You're new, unfamiliar and changing things up, so I have to start all over with my recon. You're one huge pain in my ass. That fucking fly that lands in my ice-cold drink right when I sit down and get comfortable.

I couldn't hate you more if I tried, and we're only on Rule Four.

Every single day I've been the father of a little girl, God has gotten a chuckle, watching me navigate my way through the ultimate test with which he blessed me. I've passed, with flying colors, with every breath I've taken, since the day she was born.

Are *you* man enough to pass *my* tests?

I seriously fucking doubt it.

RULE #5:
Levels of Intimacy— The Ones You'll Never Reach

Don't fucking touch my daughter.

Personally, I think that pretty much covers it, but again with the dickheads in my Crew... all still running at their sucks about how I'm being unrealistic. May I just point out, that of these buddies of mine:

One has no kids.

One has no daughter.

And the last one — secretly agrees with every word I'm saying but gets his panties bunched up anytime I speak out loud, or in this case, write it down. *And*, bastard hasn't had to deal with the burden that is you in real life, because his oldest daughter married a man we all helped raise, *the right way*, and he's actually convinced himself that his youngest is only aware of men that exist in her family, her books, or are umping a softball game.

They have no idea what I'm going through.

Just sayin'.

But, in the interest of... yeah, I got nothing... I really just want them to shut the hell up — here's a more detailed description of what's acceptable and what's a death wish for you.

*Hand Holding. I'm okay with this; how much damage could you possibly do by holding her hand? Now say "thank you," and *don't* abuse the privilege, because this is the *only* thing your fingers are to be used for and I'm being *very* generous here. I'm not even close to playin' with you when I say, I *will* slice them off, one at a time, if they wander.

*Kissing. I can't believe I'm saying this, but I'm okay with this too. Slow your roll there, hornball, this *only* applies to her hand or mouth. No slippin' over to the neck or ear. As far as you're concerned, my child has no neck or ears. And if you have Herpes Simplex *any damn number* or Mono, then don't touch her at all, not even the hand-holding. You're a disease infested vermin and need to be quarantined.

*Any State of Undress. Just. Fuck. No. I'm not even gonna explain far enough to have to say "naked," because that's no longer a word in your vocabulary. I'm talking like ten steps back from the aforementioned word you dare not think. There is *nothing* under her shirt, pants, shorts, tank top, skirt, leggings, jeggings, sweater, or any other article of top layer clothing I might've forgotten to mention, that she needs you to "check on" for *ANY* reason. Nothing.

She's been dressing and undressing herself for a long ass time, so she's more than capable of managing the perils of snaps, zippers and buttons. She doesn't need your "help" with any of it. Should she somehow find herself "trapped" inside her clothes, she knows how to dial 911, so no need for you to worry.

And the same goes for you — if you don't know how to dress and undress yourself by now, you're a fucking moron. Get gone before I help ya.

*Four on the Floor. I'm referring to each of your two feet — try to follow along now — 2 (her feet) + 2 (your feet) = 4. Keep 'em on the damn floor. What's the point of this, you ask? More than happy to tell ya! With all feet on the floor, it's damn near impossible to assume a compromising position. This eliminates any lying on backs, climbing on top of each other or straddling. Even leaning too far over a console, one foot's bound to come up... and you're now in direct violation of Rule 5, Section Four. There are several other scenarios this prohibits, but the mere thought of describing them makes me want to tear off your head and shit down your neck, so — just keep yourself in check.

*Sex. Do you *want* to die?

I think now would be an excellent time for a review, a step back to look at the whole picture in one big bang. (Coincidentally, "bang" is the sound a gun makes... just sayin'.)

At this point, you're only on Rule 5 and so far, here's what you're facing:

*You have to come to my house, get past the handshake in which I crush your metacarpals, then sit down across from me and look me in the eye as I lay out for you everything I have, by that point, dug up in your background and dissected like a blood-thirsty forensic scientist.

And then, you have to explain, in your big boy voice, anything I found and/or have questions about. And let's not forget — dependent on my findings — I may be taking you out for a driving lesson!

On the off-chance you don't run out crying in your piss-soaked pants by this point, you have to be asking yourself... is the rest *really* worth it?

Sawyer Beckett's Guide for ~~Fools~~ Tools Looking to Date My Daughter

You must have my princess home by midnight, and you don't get to stay. When you take her out, you must act more as a bodyguard than date, dance like an idiot if needed, *and* spring for valet service, all while holding your urine.

You might've had to "rehome" your pot plants and find a new job... and you only get to hold her hand or kiss her.

Think about it — you're now facing a life of being a sober, overworked, paranoid, *unlaid* asshat, being constantly watched by the father of an *only* female child, who's *never* going to like you.

If you can't fully comprehend what a grim outlook this is, lemme clear it up for you — it's gonna fucking suck!

No lie — if you actually turn the page, I'll be forced to ask myself — is this kid really as stupid as I've assumed all along, some sort of masochist who *wants* his ass beat... or could it be possible I need back-up?

RULE #6:
The Nine Lives of Dumbass (← - you)

I did it, I called in back-up. Let's face it, they would've "inserted" themselves into the investigation anyway, so why not make it seem like my idea?

Thing is — when you get close to P, you unknowingly just got close with her *whole* family. Lemme guess, you thought she just had two parents and no siblings, easy, right?

Wrong.

Surprise, shitsack! My girl's got a whole Crew and Squad of badasses who love and always stand beside her. And conveniently, can also sniff out mediocrity like bloodhounds. And the best part? Now that I've officially enlisted their help, not only do you have to worry about me, but you have to endure the scrutiny of NINE of them. Nine, hand-selected family members who each bring a different, hella appreciated, card of expertise to the table.

I'm actually a lil' scared for you, so we'll start ya out slow and build up to the heavy-hitters. No really... one of them is literally going to bring a bat. But don't worry, she's "softened" with age.

Interview 1&2: Will be conducted by... I can't use real names, so we'll just call them "Shorty" and "Songbird." These two will, *by far*, be your easiest interviews, and I've rolled them into one, because honestly, together or apart, they're both about as scary as baby kittens dressed in lil' pink coats. I have to give them a turn though or I'll never hear the end of it, so I suggest you use this time to try to win them over. They're not mean, but they *are* picky, so not a total cakewalk.

Sawyer Beckett's Guide for ~~Fools~~ Tools Looking to Date My Daughter

If they decide you deserve a chance, which short of you announcing you worship Satan or flashing a Swastika tattoo, they will — you may proceed to your next interrogation.

Interview 3&4: I'm also sending these two men in together, in the interest of efficiency, because they're basically the exact same person... the father/son tag team of "gentlemen at their finest." You won't be drilled with questions in this session either. No, the purpose here is for *them* to tell *you* how a lady should be treated. The younger guy, a Crew baby himself, just married another Crew baby, so if anyone knows the expectations of being a part of the life of one of our own — it's him. Soak up every sappy word they say, remember it, apply it... because they can teach you all that sweet shit that never even crosses my mind, and my daughter deserves the sweet shit.

Interview 5: *Uncle Z.* You're damn lucky you've got your eye on Princess P or you'd be in serious danger right about now. Z loves my child like his own, but everyone knows what he thinks is his secret — his real "soft spot" belongs to the very youngest Crew baby girl... and if it was *her* you were after, well, the big behemoth staring at you now would be maiming you. This guy will be very blunt and diplomatic with you. He'll tell you what he expects and you'll either agree or be excused. He'll ask you a bunch of questions, cool and calm as can be, that you'll either answer correctly or you won't.

I *absolutely* trust his opinion and if you're a "no" for him, you're a fucking no.

But, considering P's age and this particular uncle's annoying habit of rationalization, you'll probably make it through.

Sawyer Beckett's Guide for ~~Fools~~ Tools Looking to Date My Daughter

Interview 6: Consider this your "warm-up" spar to the big fight, 'cause it's an uphill climb to the Terror Dome from here out. This kid is one of my favorite people in the world, because he reminds me so much of myself, but more so... he reminds me of his dad (who you'll meet next and that will not go well for you.) J here will joke with ya, lure you in 'til you feel safe, like you're just talking to "one of the guys," then HOLY SHITSTORM — he'll throttle you into a big ole' pile of pussy if you say one disrespectful or questionable thing about his Squad sister. Kid's a player himself, probably not a "Dad Favorite," so I'm really just sending him in to fuck with ya.

Interview 7: And I slowly lower the boom. You think *I'm* overprotective? Welcome to the Asylum, dickstick. Mr. K here is gonna make you question everything you *thought* I'd already covered. For instance, when I grazed upon what kind of car you drove, and it not being too small and dangerous? This fucker is literally going to go check the pressure in your tires and call the dealership to ask about your airbags. He's going to make you demonstrate how to swing open a door — after all, it was his wife that taught us all the trick in the first place. Don't be surprised if he hands you a map, with the places he does and does not deem safe for a date clearly marked. He may very well bring in a doctor, or two, to draw blood, and urine samples, as well as test your IQ. And that machine you're strapped to? Yep, that is indeed a polygraph, and he's having the results read *as* you speak. Barely able to swallow down that lump of "what the hell did I get myself into" clogging your throat? We'll buckle up, Buttercup... 'cause you're not done.

Interview 8&9: You are so fucked. There's not even a word for the level of fuckedness you've just entered. I sent in #8, the redhead, for your protection, because #9, the blonde carrying the bat... say hello to my heaviest hitter. Leaving you alone with Gidget just wouldn't be fair, so, you're welcome. I'm not a complete asshole.

Red's pretty reasonable now that's she's, never mind, none of your business. Quit pryin', punk! Anyway, the ginger's gonna be searching for the good in you, probably "reading your aura" or some shit, but her main purpose is to counter-balance Mama Crew, who I'm guessin' is tapping her bat against her palm, circling you like a vulture right about now.

God help you if you don't have at least a basic knowledge of at least one sport, or haven't played one at some point in your life. Even Pee-Wee t-ball, and you were the bat boy, *anything*... I'd speak up.

She'll let ya slide on the Disney trivia, 'cause you're a guy, but she'll *still* ask. Any answer you can pop out might score you a bonus point. And by some miracle you can take any one of the classics (her words, not mine) and speak on the "life lesson" it taught... it'd be a game changer for ya. It *might* persuade her to set down the bat, no shit.

Then there's music. You better pray your musical appreciation extends beyond today's Top 40 or death metal. *If* you can play an instrument, I'd advise you to demonstrate immediately. And any old songs or bands your parents taught you, I'd start spitting into the conversation as quickly as possible.

Oh, and the smartass quips she keeps throwin' out? You stand a 50/50 chance here; truly, you're walking an invisible line between being witty enough to keep up or being a disrespectful bastard with an attitude.

Ah fuck. I'm laughing just picturing it. She's "shit your pants" scary, right? That's why we all love her. You mess with what's hers, which P is, and you'll wish you were never born. The real kicker? She's married to the crazed psycho who tortured you in interview seven, and he worships the ground she walks on, so if you offend her in any way... yeah, they won't print the book if I tell you what will happen.

Now how much fuckin' fun was *THAT*? I know I had a great time, and I wasn't even there.

If, after I consult with my comrades and they green light me to proceed, and you haven't already gone into hiding, in another country... we move on to Rule Seven.

My favorite number...

RULE #7:
WTF

Seven is *my* number, it's always been my number, and I was ready to really lay into you on this one. I had a final list of really important things we still needed to hit upon, like how pulling up with your music blaring, or God help you, *honking* to beckon my daughter's attention, would not be in your best interest. Or the way you dress. As in, if I can see your underwear because your jeans sag, I'm using the waistband of them to lift and hurl you through the air by. And that's just the beginning; my list was long. I'll never stop adding to my list.

But then, during what I can only assume was the early onset of a stroke, "they" actually convinced me to give you a chance. I can't be sure, it all happened so fast, lots of bull-headed females all squawking at once, my boys laughing at me... utter chaos ensued and here we are. The one thing I did hear loud and clear? The woman whose body I like having full access to said, "Enough. My turn to talk." I'd translate what that *really* means, but I don't wanna put any ideas of that nature in your head.

So Rule Seven has now become my best attempt at translating, and conveying to you, all the frilly, girly feedback that I was *persuaded* to add, 'cause apparently the Ovarian Council has spoken and the consensus is: you're gonna be around a while. And the following items are as, if not more, important than everything I covered.

So says the Council anyway.

*She is right. Guess I figured you already knew this; P wouldn't be lookin' at you twice if she didn't already get the vibe that you subscribe to this philosophy. But *I* learned long ago that my woman *is* always right... and she told me to add it. So there ya go.

Women can live without us a lot easier than we can live without them. If they get mad, they can call a girlfriend and tell them all about how bad we hurt them, what insensitive jerks we are, how we don't understand them, blah, blah, blah. But we don't have that option, 'cause no man wants to listen to another man whine like a pussy, so... let her be right. Especially you, since we all know in *your* case, you *are* wrong — my P's brilliant.

*Think before you speak. I *definitely* didn't write this one. More often than not, when I talk, people's jaws drop, at least one person slaps me upside the head and sometimes we get asked to leave places. The church still won't let me come back. But word on the street, the "street" being the Crew women, is that once you say something, you can never *unsay* it, and even if she *says* she forgives you... she'll never forget. This part I actually know first-hand is true, because I can be fighting with my woman about... *anything*, that happened *this year*, and all of a sudden she's crying because I said she overreacted about something I don't even remember that happened ten years ago.

Basic rule of thumb on this one? If you're mad, don't talk. If you *think* you have a valid point or argument... you don't, so don't talk. And under no circumstance *ever*, do you answer any questions about clothing, makeup, a new hairdo or weight with anything but a nod and smile. *Ever.* Just nod and smile.

*The Little Things. When they said this, I assumed they were talking about your dick and was about to kibosh the whole convo, since as far as my daughter's concerned, you don't even have a dick, no matter how little it is... but turns out, they meant something else.

As I write this, they're literally composing their own quiz for you — what are P's favorites; color, food, song, flower, perfume, and God knows what else. And dates — get familiar with the calendar on your phone — 'cause you're fully expected to remember the endless list of "moments" that somehow count as anniversaries. First kiss, first date, birthday, Valentine's, when her astrological sign aligns with yours, the first time you saw her in that one blue dress and the day you met her dog... good fuckin' luck. I'm not even sure what the penalty for an infraction in this area is because my Shorty is a realist and doesn't come at me with this shit. She knows a lost cause when she sees one. Plus, Gidget reminds me of the biggies... and we don't have a dog.

*Grandparent Rights.** I'd like to go on record as saying, if you read my rules, there's no way possible for this to ever be an issue, but Shorty's standing over my shoulder right now making me include it. Should you be "the one," and Immaculate Conception decides to grace you and my daughter... after about ten years of marriage... nope, still not on board with this horseshit.

And there it was... that slap upside my head I mentioned earlier.

Anyway, under *extreme* duress, I'm supposed to inform you of this old saying—

"A son is a son till he gets a wife, but a daughter is a daughter the rest of your life."

According to my better half (still standing here), this means — she is the "First Grandma." This title comes with the following privileges:

*Besides P and yourself, my wife gets to hold any and all babies *FIRST*. (I'm estimating this to be within ten minutes of birth.)

*Grandchildren come to our house first for holidays, birthdays, sleepovers and any other activity First Grandma deems fit. *Your* parents schedule around *us*. So basically, if our Christmas dinner starts at noon... your parents' starts the day after.

*We get first choice of seating at recitals, ball games, school ceremonies and any other activity First Grandma deems fit.

*We get the first pick of pictures taken; size, pose, etc. This applies to *all* pictures: private shoots, school, sports, etc.

*We choose what we're called first, i.e. "Nana" or "Mimi" (basically whatever my woman can get the baby to say first) and your parents may choose from the leftover "Meemaws" and the likes.

We (she) reserve the right to add to this list at any time.

I reserve the right to dismember you and bury the various parts across several counties if this rule ever becomes applicable.

And that's it. We're done. The seven rules to *try* and date my Princess.

I'm hoping that you're shaking your head, about to throw this book away and pack to move... to Honduras.

But, if you truly make my daughter happy, then I'm hoping you listened. Took notes. Made index study cards. Because honestly, I'd much rather have taught you how to ensure her endless smile than have to actually kill you.

I do want you scared, aware, always on your toes... but not actually just for my enjoyment... my real goal, concern, greatest wish in life, is her ultimate happiness and safety.

It was, is, and will always be, about her.

(If I didn't say it before, that's ^ a rule too.)

In Closing

"Women are meant to be loved, not to be understood." — Oscar Wilde

Consider me your personal Oscar Wilde.

I welcome any follow-up questions you have. If you're unsure, ask me.

Any time, day or night, if it concerns my daughter... I will answer.

ABOUT THE
AUTHOR

S.E.Hall, lover of all things anticipation and romance, is the author of The Evolve Series: Emerge, Embrace, Entangled, Entice. Baby Mama Drama and Endure, as well as the stand-alone novels Pretty Instinct and Pretty Remedy. Her co-written works included The Provocative Professions Collection: Stirred Up, Packaged and Handled, One Naughty Night and full-length novel Matched with Angela Graham as well as Conspire, a romantic suspense with Erin Noelle.

S.E. resides in Arkansas with her husband of 18 years and 3 daughters of the home. When not writing or reading, she can be found "enthusiastically cheering" on one of her girls' softball games.

Newsletter: http://eepurl.com/7E-nP

Facebook: https://www.facebook.com/S.E.HallAuthorEmerge

Amazon: http://www.amazon.com/S.E.-Hall/e/B00D0AB9TI/

Twitter: https://twitter.com/Emergeauthor

Instagram: https://www.instagram.com/sehall_author

Sawyer Beckett's Guide for ~~Fools~~ Tools Looking to Date My Daughter

The Evolve Series

Emerge: myBook.to/Emerge (FREE)

Embrace: myBook.to/Embrace

Entangled: myBook.to/Entangled

Entice: myBook.to/Entice

Sawyer Beckett's Baby Mama Drama Guide For Dummies: myBook.to/BabyMamaDrama

Endure: myBook.to/Endure